BEASTQUEST

→ BOOK FIVE ←

TARTOK
THE ICE BEAST

ADAM BLADE

ILLUSTRATED BY EZRA TUCKER

A
LITTLE APPLE
PAPERBACK

SCHOLASTIC INC.

New York Toronto London Auckland Sydney
Mexico City New Delhi Hong Kong Buenos Aires

With special thanks to Stephen Cole
To Karen, for all she's done on the Quest

ISBN-13: 978-0-439-02457-0
ISBN-10: 0-439-02457-9

Beast Quest series created by Working Partners Ltd., London.
BEAST QUEST is a trademark of Working Partners Ltd.

All rights reserved. Published by Scholastic Inc., 557 Broadway, New York, NY 10012, by arrangement with Working Partners Ltd.

12 11 10 9 8 7 6 5 4 3 2 1   7 8 9 10 11 12/0

Designed by Tim Hall
Made in China
First printing, December 2007

Reader,

Welcome to Avantia. I am Aduro — a good wizard residing in the palace of King Hugo. You join us at a difficult time. Let me explain. . . .

It is laid down in the Ancient Scripts that the peaceful kingdom of Avantia would one day be plunged into danger by the evil wizard, Malvel.

That time has come.

Under Malvel's evil spell, six Beasts — fire dragon, sea serpent, mountain giant, night horse, ice beast, and winged flame — run wild and destroy the land they once protected.

The kingdom is in great danger.

The Scripts also predict an unlikely hero. They say that a young boy shall take up the Quest to free the beasts and save the kingdom.

We pray this young boy will take up the Quest. Will you join us as we wait and watch?

Avantia salutes you,
Aduro

BLOOD ON ICE

ALBIN TOOK THE LEATHER SATCHEL FROM HIS back and kneeled down beside a small patch of dirt and rock peeking through the ice. Gently, he began to work the rock free, careful not to damage what might be beneath.

As a young boy, Albin had learned the ways of the ice. He knew that the sun would heat the exposed rocks. And that around and underneath the warmed rocks, moss, lichen, and other plants would grow. His father and others could take these mosses and make them into medicine. He had seen wounded men, sick children, and frost-weary travelers restored to health by these plants.

And he had felt their healing powers for himself —
a few years ago, a deadly fever had threatened his
life. The moss medicine saved him.

It was Albin's first time collecting without the
elders, and he was determined not to come home
empty-handed. He started in right away, pulling
up stones as he went and surveying the ground
below. Albin's cousin, Oskie, walked nearby,
kicking roughly at the occasional rock and checking
hastily underneath it. But Albin was too focused
on his own task to notice.

Underneath one of the larger stones, Albin
found something. The bright green lichen on the
underside of the rock was among the rarest.
The medicine it made was strong — one plant
would be able to save many lives.

"Over here!" Albin called to his cousin.

"What is it?" Oskie asked lazily. He was lying on
his back nearby, watching the long, wispy clouds
in the sky.

"Look at this!" Albin pointed to what he had found. "A healing herb."

Oskie got up slowly and came over. Together, the boys carefully pulled the lichen from the rock. It came off in long strips that they rolled into tight coils. When they finished with that stone, they turned over another, larger one.

Under the next rock was even more of the healing herb. The boys worked quickly. It was already late in the afternoon, and they would have to return to their village before it got too dark.

As he adjusted to the rhythm of the work — overturning rocks, pulling up the moss, and storing it in the satchel — Albin forgot to stay aware of his surroundings. The first rule of the ice is to always know where you are and what is around you.

Suddenly alarmed, Albin looked up from the rock. He surveyed the hard, icy landscape stretching out into the distance, glimmering under the burnt orange of the setting sun. Satisfied that things were safe, he went back to work.

Finishing with that rock, he moved to the next.

"Oskie, help me turn this stone," he said to his cousin. But there was no reply. "Oskie?"

Albin turned around to see what Oskie was doing. Expecting to see his cousin daydreaming again, he was surprised to find him standing with a rigid, terrified look on his face.

"What is it, Oskie?" Albin asked.

"There! In the distance —" Oskie stammered, fear in his voice.

On the horizon, drawing near, was a towering creature. Its shaggy fur was thick and dark, and stood out against the white of the icy plains. Blood-red eyes glared at the boys, and its huge, curving claws sliced through the air. Drooling jaws snapped open to reveal stained, yellow fangs.

Albin was too scared even to scream. He slowly backed away, pulling his cousin with him. Dragging his eyes away from the monster's jaws, Albin saw it wore a glowing collar around its neck. The fur there had been clawed away to reveal raw pink flesh.

The monster stamped one massive paw down on the ice. Sparks seemed to dance around it, and the shockwave jarred every bone in Albin's body. The cousins tried to scramble away, but the ice was cracking all around them. Huge gaps began to open as the boys tried desperately to get away from the roaring Beast.

Albin was too slow. The monster's claws swiped against his side, tearing through his thick clothes. He gripped his side in pain and fell to the ground. But the Beast wasn't finished with him yet. The next blow sent Albin sliding toward a huge crack in the ice.

Oskie flung himself toward Albin. But the ice was slippery, and Oskie couldn't hold on for long. Together, the cousins went tumbling into the dark abyss under the ice.

CHAPTER ONE

QUEST TO THE NORTH

"Of all the places our Beast Quest has taken us," Tom said, "this must be the most incredible!" He stared out at the icy plains. They stretched into the distance under a sky of vivid blue.

"It's so open," Elenna agreed, pulling her shawl tightly around her. "It looks as if the ice goes on forever." In one direction, the ice plains seemed to disappear into the horizon. On the other side, snow-capped mountains rose like sharp teeth biting into the sky.

Tom smiled at his friend. Something about the landscape felt magical. Elenna smiled back. Her pet wolf, Silver, pressed up to her, his shiny gray fur speckled with snow. She looked grateful for the warmth of his body against her legs.

"I'll check the map and see how much farther we have to go," Tom said. He pulled the well-worn scroll from the saddlebag of his stallion, Storm. The horse stood like a dark shadow against the whiteness all around, and gave a soft nicker as Tom patted his neck.

"We're close to the northern edge of Avantia. We'll need to go eastward soon." Tom pointed to the red path on the map that showed their route. It glowed and pulsed on the parchment paper.

This was no ordinary map. It was a magical map given to them by the wizard Aduro. It guided Tom and Elenna on their quest to rid the kingdom of a deadly threat.

The Beasts.

All his life, Tom had heard stories of the Beasts

that dwelled in the deepest corners of the kingdom of Avantia — dragons, sea serpents, horse-men, and giants, just to name a few. Growing up with his aunt and uncle, he used to think they were fairy tales. He'd certainly never seen a Beast. But then he'd never laid eyes on his father Taladon, either, and Tom believed he'd meet him one day.

Now he knew that the Beasts were real. And a dark wizard named Malvel had enslaved them. He was using them to spread terror and destruction across the land for his own evil ends. King Hugo of Avantia and his wizard, Aduro, had chosen Tom to go on a special quest to set the Beasts free and save the kingdom.

Tom had set off with only Storm, his sword, and his shield for protection. But soon he had met Elenna and Silver, who had joined him on his Quest. Without them, Tom knew he would never have made it this far.

"We'd better get going," said Elenna, studying

the map. Tall and thin, she had messy black hair, large brown eyes, and a smile full of warmth — even in the freezing cold of the northern plains. "Looks like there's a small shelter for travelers an hour's trek from here. We can stay the night there before continuing on. I'm so tired I could sleep standing up!"

"Me, too," said Tom. Leading Storm along by his halter, Tom began trudging across the ice once more. He noticed a large bundle of green leaves sprouting up from the icy ground. "Hey, look at that plant. It must be hardy to survive out here."

"A lot of plants used in medicine are found in the mountains and gullies around here," Elenna told him. "The nomads collect them and supply the kingdom."

Tom fingered the key he kept around his neck, the key that could set the Beasts free. *There are so many dangers here*, he thought. *The nomads won't survive long without Tartok's protection.* A sharp

gust of wind blew up suddenly, making him shiver. He quickened his step. "Come on, the sooner we're somewhere dry and warm the better."

Silver yapped suddenly. "He agrees with us," Elenna joked uneasily. Then she crouched beside him. "Silver? What's wrong?"

Tom saw the wolf's eyes narrow. A growl was building in the back of Silver's throat. "Perhaps he can smell something," he said.

"Or sense something," said Elenna, concern in her voice. She looked around, trying to see what was bothering the wolf. The sky had now grown dark and the air was much colder. It felt like a storm was moving in.

A strong gust of wind whipped at their clothes. Instead of dying down though, it only grew stronger. Tiny shards of snow and ice stung Tom's skin. Elenna's shawl was almost ripped away by the sudden gale.

"I can't believe how quickly the weather has

changed," Elenna said. "A moment ago the skies were clear."

"Not anymore," Tom shouted over the wind. Now the sky overhead was dark gray and wild with snow. Storm plunged forward, and Tom stroked his head. "We must keep going and reach that shelter."

"How can we?" Elenna clung to her shawl. "The map's useless if we can't see any landmarks!"

Tom knew she was right. Worse still, with the sun blotted out by the snow and clouds, they had no way of getting their bearings. "I think east was this way," said Tom, turning into the gray haze, trying not to panic. The stinging snow was blowing so hard he could barely keep his eyes open. "Or was it the other way?"

"I'm not sure," said Elenna as the storm grew fiercer around them. "We have to find shelter quickly or we won't stand a chance!"

CHAPTER TWO

A SIGHTING ON THE ICE

"WE MUST KEEP MOVING," SAID TOM. "IF WE stand still we will freeze to death." Tom had faced so many dangers on his Quest — he wasn't about to be defeated by a snowstorm. He took hold of Storm's bridle and led him through the driving snow. Elenna walked at Storm's side, one arm thrown over his back, hugging him for warmth and support. Silver ran around between them, barking.

"I can't see a thing!" Elenna shouted.

"Just keep holding on to Storm!" Tom yelled back, but the wind seemed to whip the words from his mouth before they could be heard. Already his body was turning numb. Desperately, he broke into a stumbling run — then gasped as he hit something solid.

"What is it?" Elenna screamed over the wind.

"I've led us into a snowdrift!" he exclaimed. *Now what?* But then Silver pushed past him and started burrowing at the huge mound of snow. Tom felt a surge of hope go through him. "Of course! We could dig —"

"— a snow cave!" cried Elenna. She started to claw at the packed snow.

"Wait," said Tom, swinging his shield from his back. It was a charmed shield — every time he released a Beast, he gained a new magical power. It could protect him from fire, save him from drowning or falling from great heights, and it could even give him extra speed. But now, he could use it as a shovel!

He began to dig into the snowdrift with the edge of the shield. As the snow tumbled away, Silver helped by working at the drift with his heavy paws. Elenna pulled Tom's sword from his belt and started chopping at the parts that were too solid to dig into. "It'll need to be a big cave for all four of us!" she shouted.

"The work will help us keep warm," Tom yelled back. "Make sure to pile the snow behind us. It will act as a windbreak."

They continued to dig into the snowdrift, packing down the sides and roof as they went. The snow they piled outside cut down on the wind and kept more snow from blowing in.

At last, Tom and Elenna had carved enough space to form a small shelter that would protect them from the worst of the weather. They crawled inside and sat down, hugging their knees to their chests. It was dark and cold, and they huddled together for warmth with Silver between them.

"Come on, Storm," Tom said to his horse. The stallion could fit only his front quarters inside, so

Tom covered Storm's back end with blankets. When the horse lay down, he blocked the entrance and helped keep out the blizzard. Storm rested his muzzle on Tom's shoulder and snorted softly. Tom and Elenna looked at each other.

"It's the best we can do," Tom muttered.

They sat uneasily in silence, listening to the wind howling outside.

Eventually, the roar of the storm dimmed to background noise. Once in a while, a strong gust would blow some snow in, but for the most part, they were warm and safe.

"I wonder how long it will last," Elenna said, her voice trembling with worry.

"I don't know." Tom didn't want to scare his friend, but he knew that storms in the North could last for days, sometimes weeks. He felt a flash of panic — they would starve to death if the storm lasted that long. Was this how Tom's father, Taladon, had disappeared? A victim of the elements? Tom shuddered at the thought. He had never met his father, who had vanished not long after Tom was born. Tom hoped the Beast Quest would make his father proud. But what if Taladon wasn't even around to hear about Tom's triumphs? Tom pushed the thought from his mind.

As the hours passed, Tom felt himself getting tired. The blowing wind began to lull him to sleep. Seeing that Elenna was already snoring softly and knowing that there was nothing he could do about the storm, Tom closed his eyes.

He awoke with a start. How long had he been asleep? He looked around the snow cave. Everyone was gone!

Tom rushed to the cave's entrance and popped his head out. He was blinded by a bright sun high in the sky.

"Well, good afternoon, sleepyhead!" Elenna said cheerfully. She was kneeling beside Silver, petting

her companion. "We didn't want to wake you because we know you need your sleep!"

"I don't believe it," said Tom, patting Storm on the neck. "I was worried the storm might never end."

"We got lucky," Elenna said with a weary smile.

Tom brushed some snow away from Storm's legs. "Come on. The sooner we reach that shelter —"

"Actually, I think there might be something closer," said Elenna, pointing toward a tall spike of ice in the distance.

Shielding his eyes from the blinding glare of the snow, Tom saw what she was looking at — a ramshackle collection of tents clustered in the hollow of the icy peak. Some tents were short and squat, others tapering and tall — but all were protected from the strong winds. It was a good place for a miniature city built from sticks and animal skins.

"What's that?" Tom wondered.

"Nomads," said Elenna. "The people Tartok is meant to protect, remember? This must be one of their camps."

"Then let's get going," said Tom. "Maybe they've seen Tartok. Maybe they know where we can find her —"

"And maybe they will have hot drinks, dry blankets, and a bed for the night!" Elenna turned and strode off toward the camp, Silver bounding after her. But, suddenly, both stopped dead in their tracks.

"What is it?" called Tom, running over. Storm trotted along beside him.

Elenna turned to him. "We may not be the first ones to come visiting that camp. Something's been here before us."

She pointed to a giant footprint in the ice, one filled with water! The deep indentations in the snow clearly outlined pads and claws. It was the footprint of an enormous creature — the first of a trail, leading toward the distant camp.

Elenna kneeled to trace a finger around the edge of the print. She shivered and stood back up. Tom gazed out at the horizon. Empty — or that's the way it looked.

"The Ice Beast," Tom whispered, gripping the hilt of his sword.

CHAPTER THREE

ENCOUNTER ON THE PLAINS

TOM, ELENNA, AND THE ANIMALS FOLLOWED the footprints until the snow became solid ice and they disappeared.

"Which way did Tartok go?" wondered Elenna. "Do you think she reached the camp?"

"Since it's still standing, probably not," said Tom.

With no trail left to follow, they pressed on toward the camp, skidding and sliding along the treacherous ice. Shallow pools of melted water flared as bright as flames as they caught the rays of the evening sun. Storm wasn't happy to be on such a slippery surface. His hooves seemed unable to find a grip.

"I know it's bad," Tom said to Storm, "but just keep going." Tom looked up to see how much farther they had to go. He shielded his eyes and squinted — not too far. But something — or someone — was headed their way. "Look there!" Tom called to Elenna. It was a horse-drawn sleigh speeding toward them over the ice, drawn by a handsome blond horse.

It was driven by a man wrapped warmly in animal skins and a fur hat. He steered the horse with a long set of reins. "Whoa," he called out. The horse obediently came to a halt, his hooves skidding slightly on the ice. As the man rose up from the sleigh, the horse whinnied to Storm.

"Greetings," the man said. "I am Brendan, the Chief of my clan."

Tom held out his hand. "I'm Tom and this is Elenna."

"Our friends here are Silver and Storm," Elenna added. "Silver is a tame wolf. He won't harm you."

Brendan's dark eyes flicked between them. "It is unusual to find anyone traveling the northern plains. It's very dangerous out here."

Tom hesitated to explain himself. The king had made him swear to keep his Quest secret. But he didn't like lying. Instead, he said nothing.

Brendan looked him over once more, but asked no questions. It was a custom of the northern people to respect a person's silence.

"Are you in need of shelter?" Brendan asked.

Both Tom and Elenna nodded.

"We have traveled a long way and we are very tired," Tom said.

Brendan nodded. "You can stay with us until you are rested enough to continue your journey — whatever that may be."

With Tom riding Storm, Elenna riding with Brendan, and Silver keeping pace beside them, the group began to make their way toward the camp. After a short distance, Brendan halted his sleigh and got out. He crouched down beside a small patch of green, fleshy leaves.

"This will help you." He paused, carefully pulling up the plant. Tom climbed down from Storm's saddle to get a closer look. Its roots were white and straggly. "This is a kind of seaweed able to grow in ice. It helps to reduce fever in those who are sick, and restores warmth to those who've stayed too long on the open ice. We have built a camp on the coast so we can harvest it. We keep what we need and trade the rest for supplies. That is how we live."

"Seaweed? So we've been walking over a frozen bay," Tom realized.

"Yes. And you are lucky to have made it here safely." Brendan tucked the plant into a pouch tied around his waist. "My son was attacked by a wild animal. It seems there is something loose on these plains. It's not safe for anyone out here," said Brendan. "These are harsh lands. And harsh times, too." He glanced over at the orange sun. "Nature is restless."

Tom and Elenna exchanged looks. *It's not just nature that is restless*, thought Tom. With Malvel's evil spell, Tartok was now a threat to the very people she was meant to protect.

Tom forced a smile and patted his horse's side for comfort, before climbing onto his back to continue their trek.

Overhead, the sky was darkening.

→ Chapter Four ←

TERROR BY NIGHT

As Tom guided Storm through the camp, he saw people wrapped in furs and skins going about their business: sorting herbs, rinsing them, and drying them over fires.

Once they were settled, Elenna changed into borrowed clothes made from tough leather.

"I can't remember the last time I felt this warm and dry!" she said, pressing a bundle of clothes into his arms. "Here are some for you, too. Oh, Tom, everyone here seems so kind. Brendan is even making room for Storm in the stables."

"When I said I'd make you comfortable, I meant all of you!" came Brendan's voice.

"We're really grateful," Tom said, as Brendan turned the corner, approaching them with a young boy of about eight or nine.

"This is my son, Albin," Brendan said, "the one who was attacked on the ice."

"It's nice to meet you, Albin," Elenna said to the boy. "We're glad that you're okay."

"Yes," Tom said. "Did it get you pretty bad?"

Albin lifted his woolen tunic to reveal three deep gashes in his side.

"He was lucky," Brendan said. "These lands aren't safe any longer." He looked at Tom and Elenna, and his face softened. "You are welcome to camp with us as long as you like. But if you stay, we ask that you do your share around the camp."

"You can help me peel the vegetables," said Albin brightly. "Then the stew will be ready sooner!"

"Sounds good to me." Tom smiled. "I'll get Storm settled for the night, then I'll join you."

Tom crossed to the stables and quickly changed into his dry clothes. Then he picked up an armful of sweet-smelling hay and placed it in Storm's stall.

"See you in the morning," he said.

Storm whinnied softly and watched as Tom left the stall to find Elenna. She and Albin were in the cooking tent, scraping the skins from a pile of vegetables with sharp stones. A rich, salty smell was rising from a bubbling cauldron tended by an old woman and a gaggle of small children.

"Shame that monster didn't leave one of its claws behind," Albin was saying. "Would have peeled these much faster."

"You're very brave. It must have been scary," Tom said casually, joining in the work.

"A little bit," the boy said, trying his best to appear brave and calm. "It was huge. Its eyes were redder than blood."

"It sounds terrifying," said Elenna.

"And it made a horrible noise — a roar louder than the wind." Albin shuddered at the memory.

"Where did you see it?" asked Tom.

"In the snow dunes out toward the Rolaz Crossing," the boy answered.

"Could you show us sometime?" Tom prodded.

Albin looked right at him, and now Tom could see the fear in the boy's eyes. "I got away once. I'm not going back there again."

Night had fallen and the temperature with it. The clan gathered around the campfire to eat their meal. Tom was grateful for the warmth of the flames and the hot stew in his belly. But the mood around the fire was dark. Everyone seemed jittery.

Elenna had shared her food with Silver, and now he lay beside her, asleep. Tom wished he could find rest so easily. Albin's description of the giant monster had done nothing to ease his worries about meeting this Beast . . . but he knew that it was his destiny to face up to his fears. He would never give up.

Just then, an unearthly howl sounded close by.

Silver awoke instantly, hackles rising and teeth bared. People scrambled to their feet in a panic. Tom drew his sword, his heart pounding.

"Snow leopard!" someone cried.

"It's somewhere close by!" yelled another.

"Nobody move," Brendan bellowed. The people froze, and even Silver stopped howling. "A leopard won't attack if we stay together. But if we separate, it will go for whoever seems an easy target."

The howl came again, even closer this time.

"That's not the howl of a snow leopard," whispered Albin. "That's the monster that attacked me!"

"Ssshh . . ." Brendan urged.

And then everything went silent. Eerily silent.

→ CHAPTER FIVE ←

THE EXPEDITION

TOM SAT DEATHLY STILL, LISTENING TO THE flickering of the fire and the creaking of the tent poles in the wind. The night was quiet — too quiet. As the seconds ticked by, Tom wondered what Tartok could be planning.

Fingering the handle of his sword, Tom exchanged looks with Brendan and Elenna. If the Beast attacked, it would be up to them to defend the camp.

Then there was a loud, sharp crack. Tom bolted upright, his sword drawn. The ground began to shake violently. Tom was thrown to the ground as a thunderous crash rang out — the ice over the bay was splitting apart!

The howl came again, this time much closer.

Tom scrambled to his feet and saw the icy mountain shaking violently, its top beginning to splinter.

"Take shelter!" he yelled.

"Quick, over here!" Elenna called out from the entrance to Brendan's tent. Tom dove under the heavy canvas tarp with the others as shards of ice fell from the sky. They were surrounded by terrible sounds — shattering, smashing, snapping — and the roar of cracking ice. And above it all was the bloodcurdling howl of the monster.

Then, as suddenly as it began, everything stopped, and there was silence over the ice once again.

But nobody dared move, or sleep. As the night wore on, everyone clustered close around the dying fire. As the sky began to lighten with the rising sun, the flames flickered out. They had made it through the night.

Slowly, people began to emerge from their shelters, groggy from the sleepless night. All around, tents had been ripped apart by huge blocks of jagged ice. It was amazing that no one had been killed! And right through the center of camp ran a wide, deep crack.

Surveying the damage, the nomads seemed angry and scared. They murmured about being cursed. But Brendan's face was determined, and he called everyone to gather around.

"We must seek help," he announced. "I know of a clan living on better ground over the border in Rolaz. It is led by a woman named Jennal. I shall go to her camp and ask if she'll let us band together with her people."

An old man nodded. "There will be safety in numbers. It is a good plan."

"I will go today," Brendan went on. "It is a day's ride by sleigh, so I shall not be back until tomorrow. I would like you to come with me, Tom."

"I'll come with you, too," said Albin.

"No," said Brendan firmly.

"But Father, if anything happens to you we will all be lost!"

Brendan placed a hand on the boy's shoulder. "I think you have used up your luck, Albin. You must stay here, and that is final."

As Albin skulked away miserably, Tom looked at Brendan. "I'll go with you," Tom agreed.

"Gather what you will need for the journey," Brendan said. "We'll meet in an hour by the stables."

As Brendan left the tent, Tom smiled at Elenna.

"This is my chance to free Tartok," he whispered.

* * *

Brendan was happy that Tom had agreed to join him.

"I want to take gifts for Jennal's clan on a separate sleigh," he told Tom. "But I would prefer all the adults to stay here to help defend the camp. Have you ever driven a sleigh?"

"No," Tom admitted. "But Storm and I make a good team. We'll soon learn."

Brendan smiled. "I'm sure you will."

Tom was led to a sleigh made of bark and skins, which ran on hefty wooden runners. He sat on the driver's seat, a pile of blankets, food, and other gifts for Jennal's clan bundled up behind him. Storm needed special ridged horseshoes to help him grip the ice, and held himself patiently while the clan's blacksmith nailed them to his hooves. Tom was given lessons on how to steer a sleigh, pulling on the reins with short, measured movements.

"We should leave," Brendan announced. "But

first, I must tell you about the ice. It's important that we travel spaced apart. The ice is thin in places, and too much weight will cause it to crack. Sometimes it's just dry land underneath, but other times, it's water."

Tom nodded.

Brendan barked a command and his horse plunged forward, jerking the sleigh into motion. "Go, Storm!" shouted Tom. The stallion neighed, and a moment later, Tom's own sleigh was moving across the ice. Elenna jumped in the air, waving good-bye, and Silver barked and yapped. They were off! Tom slapped his reins against the front of the sleigh and gave a whoop of exhilaration. This is what Tom had been waiting for — to get closer to the snow monster.

Storm picked up speed, responding swiftly to Tom's commands. The sun turned the ice field blindingly bright, and the cold bite of the wind chilled Tom's cheeks. As the sleigh bumped and scraped over the ice and snow, faster and faster, Tom felt adrenaline surge through him.

They passed soft white bumps of snowdrifts and jagged icy gullies. There were dozens of places Tartok could be hiding, but Tom couldn't see any telltale footprints.

The two sleighs passed through a broad valley that rose and fell in great white sweeps. It was a struggle to keep up with Brendan, but Storm was powerful and determined. Ears flattened against the icy wind, he set such a pace that they never lost sight of the sleigh in front.

"Are you all right, Tom?" boomed Brendan, his voice echoing around the valley.

"I'm great!" Tom yelled, the wind whipping water from his eyes, his bones jolting as the sleigh careened over the uneven ground.

All around them was flat, white wilderness that seemed to stretch on forever, interrupted only by clusters of spindly trees with wide, flat leaves. The sleigh made a smooth scraping noise as they reached a frozen inlet. Tom noticed pools of water and cracks in the ice. Could they have been made by the Beast?

Tom scanned the horizon for any sign of Tartok. With a gasp of surprise, he saw another sleigh following them, some distance away. Its driver was a small, huddled figure that Tom recognized at once.

It was Albin.

"Brendan!" Tom yelled ahead, but the wind snatched the words from his mouth and Albin's father was too far in front to hear. Tom heard a thick cracking sound. Storm gave an alarmed whinny as the ice cracked beneath his hooves. Tom looked down and caught a glimpse of glittering turquoise water below. The ice had split open to reveal the sea underneath! Was the sleigh going to plunge into the icy sea?

"Whoa, Storm!" Tom shouted, and the stallion slowed to a halt. The sleigh lurched to one side, then stopped. Brendan hadn't noticed anything wrong and was drawing farther away. But Albin was still following in their wake, and if the ice was unsafe . . .

"Albin, stop!" Tom shouted, jumping out of the sleigh and waving his arms. "The ice is splitting!"

But Albin couldn't hear. Tom watched as the horse dragged the sleigh toward the weakened ice. It was too late. In an instant, the ice broke up around Albin like shattering glass. The horse snorted in terror, rearing up. The sleigh skidded out of control.

"No!" Tom cried out. He watched helplessly as Albin was thrown over the side of the sleigh into the freezing water.

CHAPTER SIX

THE RESCUE

"ALBIN!" YELLED TOM, RUNNING TO WHERE the boy had fallen. Albin had vanished from view. Tom realized he must be under the ice, trying to fight his way back up to the surface.

Tom hunted around for the tiniest flash of movement. With Albin trapped under the water, Tom knew that every second counted. He threw himself down on his knees, trying to spot some dark shadow on the other side of the ice. After what felt like forever, a shadowy blue outline appeared.

"Albin!" Tom shouted again. He leaped to his feet and pulled his sword from his side. Taking a huge breath of cold air, he struck the hilt against the ice with all his might. The ice just chipped. But Tom kept striking at it. He could see Albin underneath, struggling desperately. With a final blow, the ice shattered and Albin reared out of the water, gasping for breath and blue with cold.

"Help!" he spluttered. "Tom, please —"

"Grab hold of me!" Tom yelled. He reached for the boy's hands but Albin was flailing, splashing water everywhere as he tried to keep himself afloat.

Albin dipped under the blue water. Tom thrust his arm into the hole and cried out. It was colder than anything he had ever experienced. Within seconds he had lost all feeling in his hand, and was sweeping it numbly through the water.

Then there was a tug. It was Albin gripping on to him. Tom pulled his arm out of the water, dragging Albin up with it. "Help me, Tom!" he gasped. But he was struggling only feebly now. Tom knew that if the boy let go and went down

another time, he would not rise up again. He grabbed Albin with his other hand.

Then he felt the ice split beneath him.

Tom held his breath. He looked down and saw the angry crack running through the ice below him. Any sudden movement could split it wide open. "Hook your arm around mine. I've got you," he urged the boy.

Shivering violently in the water, Albin did as he was told. Tom was starting to shiver, too. He knew he had to get the boy out — but also knew that the ice could give way at any moment, and they would both be lost in the icy waters.

Suddenly, Tom gasped as he felt a pressure on the backs of his legs. "Hold still, Tom."

"Brendan!" Tom cried, relief flooding through him. "I — I think the ice is going to crack under me!"

"I've got you. Just don't let go of Albin, and I'll pull you both clear."

"Dad?" Albin gasped through chattering teeth. "Is that you?"

"I'm here," called Brendan. Tom felt him pull on his legs. Together they were towing Albin toward the edge of the hole in the ice. Tensing his muscles, Tom managed to drag the boy's upper body up onto the fragile ice. Then Brendan crawled over and hauled his son free of the icy water.

"Sorry, Father," Albin breathed.

"Oh, my son, my son," Brendan murmured.

"I'll fetch some blankets from the sleigh," Tom panted, his heart thumping like a sledgehammer in his chest. He grabbed a bundle and flew back across the ice. "I'm glad you came back."

"I realized you were no longer behind me, so I came looking," said Brendan, wrapping Albin in the blankets and rubbing the shivering boy's wrists to get his circulation moving. "Why did you come after me?"

"Wanted . . . to bring you . . . luck, Father," Albin stammered.

Brendan cradled his son's head and smiled warmly at Tom. "I believe this stranger has brought us both luck."

Tom smiled back through his exhaustion and staggered to the sleigh to get a blanket for himself. They would build a fire to warm up, and then they would get on their way.

Back at the sleigh, Storm nickered with concern, pressing his head against Tom's chest. Tom rubbed his numb fingers against the stallion's chestnut mane. There was a pounding in his head, and at first, Tom thought it was his racing pulse.

But the pounding was coming from somewhere else. A distant thumping sound. Not only that, but the ice was trembling faintly beneath his feet. Tom listened hard. There was another sound. The howl of something fierce.

"Tartok," he whispered.

CHAPTER SEVEN

TORN APART

HIS HEARTBEAT QUICKENING, TOM LOOKED all around him. The horizon was full of distant dunes, but there was no Beast in sight. Tom turned to see if Brendan had heard the sound. But right now, Albin was the man's only focus. Tom looked down at his feet and saw an intricate lacework of cracks spreading over the ice with every thump. He caught his breath as the hairline cracks surrounded him.

Tom knew the old stories about Tartok. The Beast was able to shatter ice with just a stamp of her foot! If she came any closer, they wouldn't stand a chance out on the open ice. As he knelt to examine the cracks, he couldn't help but remember the chill of the water below. . . .

Tom was jolted from his dark thoughts by a glimpse of movement in the distance — three dark figures on horseback, coming from the direction of the camp. And one of them appeared to be Elenna. He waved to the riders urgently. "Brendan and Albin need help!" he called. He saw the figures lean forward in their saddles, driving their horses still faster.

Elenna was first to arrive beside the upturned sleigh, two older women just behind her — Tom recognized them as Brendan's wife and her sister. They leaped from their horses and gathered around Brendan and Albin with blankets and dry clothes to keep them warm.

"I realized Albin must have gone after you," Elenna said, dismounting. "I came with his mother and aunt to bring him back."

Tom jerked his head toward his sleigh and beckoned Elenna to follow him. He looked over his shoulder to make sure no one was near. "Can you feel that vibration?" he whispered.

Elenna stood still and looked down at the maze of hairline cracks in the ice. Tom could feel the ground shift beneath his feet — and clearly so could Elenna. She gave him a fearful nod. "It's Tartok, isn't it?"

"We have to find her," said Tom, nodding slowly.

Suddenly, a huge tremor tore through the silence and a large, jagged crack appeared in the ice. Storm snorted, and Tom gasped as he was knocked to his knees.

"The ice field's breaking up!" shouted Brendan. "Quickly, Tom, Elenna — get over here!"

Tom realized that the split in the ice was threatening to divide them — Tom, Elenna,

Storm, and the sleigh on one side, and everyone else on the other. He scrambled up and started pulling at Storm's harness. "We must release him from the sleigh," Tom said urgently. "If it falls through a gap in the ice, he won't stand a chance!"

Elenna joined him, wrestling with the buckles. Brendan tried to come over to help — but the split opened wider. The ice creaked and groaned as it was torn apart. It sounded like the moan of an animal in pain — as though the ice were alive!

Brendan teetered on the edge of the divide, but just managed to fall backward to safety. One of the horses bolted and nearly trampled him as it leaped across the split, skidding onto the other side. Elenna caught hold of its bridle and hushed it, slowly bringing it back under control.

"It's no good!" Brendan shouted over to Tom and Elenna. "I can't reach you now."

Tom undid Storm's last buckle and turned to see that the brilliant turquoise split was now as wide as a river, stretching in either direction as far as the eye could see. The blue water almost looked beautiful — even though it was deadly. "Don't worry about us," said Tom. "Albin needs to get back to the camp before the ice gets any weaker."

"Head due east, to the foothills of the great ice mountain," Brendan shouted over. "You will reach Jennal's clan before nightfall. They will give you shelter. Will you explain to them what I want to do?"

"We'll try our best," Tom yelled back. "Now, don't waste any more time on us — go!"

"The horse's name is Shah," Brendan's wife called out.

Shah, a stout bay pony, had calmed down now. He pressed his muzzle against Elenna's neck and snorted softly. She turned to Tom. "Are we going to the other clan now?"

"We will," said Tom quietly. "But first we must find Tartok."

"I wish we had Silver with us," Elenna said, swinging herself up into Shah's saddle.

"He'll be able to protect the camp from any invaders," Tom reassured her. "Come on." He turned Storm toward the snow dunes. "It's time we met face-to-face, Tartok," he said. "As long as I'm alive, I'll fight the evil of Malvel."

Then, with a huge creak and boom, a fresh crack opened up in the ice right beside Shah. The pony snorted in fear and reared up, striking out with his front legs. Elenna gasped and threw herself forward, her hands clutching his mane, her feet slipping from the stirrups. Before Elenna could sit up in the saddle there was another loud crack.

Whinnying in alarm, Shah shot forward. Elenna grabbed the reins. "Whoa! Steady, boy!"

But the terrified pony plunged onward, his hooves throwing up clouds of snow as he galloped toward the distant dunes.

→→ CHAPTER EIGHT ←←

FURY ON THE ICE

TOM RAN OVER TO STORM, AND SWUNG HIMSELF onto the horse's back. "Go, boy!" Tom shouted, pressing his heels against Storm's sides.

They raced across the frozen inlet after Elenna. They came to another crack in the ice, but Storm didn't hesitate — he gathered himself and leaped forward. Tom felt the air whistle past him. It was as if they were flying! Storm's front legs reached out and landed safely on solid ice at the other side.

"Faster, boy," Tom urged — they were gaining, but not quickly enough. Elenna disappeared out of sight behind one of the snow dunes.

Her scream cut through the crisp arctic air like a knife.

"Elenna!" Tom yelled. "Hold on, I'm coming!" Storm's hooves thundered across the tundra. What had happened to Elenna to make her cry out like that?

A terrifying roar sounded from close by, together with the sound of shattering ice.

Tartok, thought Tom, fear and panic rising up from his stomach.

As Storm galloped around the side of the snow dune, Tom saw the Beast standing ahead of him in a narrow valley. The huge, shaggy monster was facing away from him — and standing over Elenna. Tartok's legs were thick with bulky muscles.

Storm skidded to a halt just a few strides from the monster. Elenna lay on her back, a trickle of blood seeping from her forehead. *Was she . . .*

could she be . . . dead? "No," he breathed. "No, she can't be —"

Tartok swung around to face him.

Even sitting high on Storm's back, Tom felt like an ant in the Beast's hulking presence. With one step, she could squash the life out of him. Her fur was dark. Her eyes were redder than a blacksmith's fire and her claws looked sharper than daggers. Her hideous face was scrunched up with anger and hate, and around her raw, welted neck was Malvel's golden collar. It glowed with an evil energy.

Tom remained still, assessing the situation.

Tartok growled and stamped a paw down on the ground. Sparks seemed to jump up from the thick ice, leaving hairline cracks etched in its surface. Clearly, she was going nowhere.

Tom climbed down from Storm's back. He wanted to make sure Elenna was okay, but first he had to free Tartok. There was no time to waste.

As if sensing the danger, Elenna regained consciousness. "What happened?" she asked groggily, opening her eyes. "Shah threw me and then —" Elenna gasped as she saw Tartok. The Beast roared, thumping her chest. The collar around her neck glowed brighter. Tartok pulled at it as if she were trying to get rid of it.

"Elenna, quick," said Tom, while the Beast was turned away from him. He pulled the wooden shield from his back, took careful aim, and slid it across the smooth ice toward her. The shield whizzed past Tartok's legs, and Elenna struggled to catch it.

Tartok roared again and brought her yellow claws swiping down — just as Elenna pulled the shield up over her head for protection. The claws wedged deep into the wood and wrenched the shield away. Tom watched in horror as Elenna stared up wide-eyed at the Beast.

Before Tom could do anything, Tartok turned and threw the shield back at him. He ducked and it whistled past, slicing into the snow. Running over the ice to reach it, he tried to pull it free, tugging on the wood with all his might. At last it came loose, but Tom couldn't stop himself from tumbling backward with it onto the snow.

An ear-splitting roar made him turn in terror. The shaggy bulk of Tartok lunged toward him, claws reaching for his throat.

CHAPTER NINE

THE PRICE OF VICTORY

Tom gasped as Tartok closed in. He dove aside as the Beast's claws ripped through the air. Sliding on the ice across the narrow valley, he crashed into the steep snow bank on the far side.

"Tom, look out!" Elenna yelled. Tom turned to find Tartok lunging toward him for a second time. He swung his shield up to protect himself. Tartok's huge paw smashed into it with enough force to knock Tom halfway through the snow dune. He heard Storm whinny with fear. His shield arm ached with pain. With a pang of terror, Tom knew Tartok was only just getting started.

"Elenna, take Storm and get out of here!" Tom

shouted quickly. The Beast stamped a huge paw down on the ice and snapped her jaws.

Then with a deep, splintering crack, the ice gave way! In an instant, she had vanished through a narrow, jagged hole into the freezing depths. Tom leaped back, almost falling in himself.

Dazed, he watched the water churn and bubble in front of him.

"Tom," cried Elenna. Storm had come to her side and she was leaning on the horse for support. "Draw your sword. Now's our chance to end this."

But as she spoke, the water exploded upward in a freezing fountain. With a roar, Tartok's head broke the surface.

Elenna ran over, trying to get the Beast's attention.

The snow monster was bobbing with her head and shoulders above the surface of the water.

Tartok turned on instinct to snap at Elenna —
giving Tom a clear view of the locked collar around
the creature's neck.

"Do it, Tom!" cried Elenna, jumping back out
of the Beast's reach.

Tom pulled the key given to him by the King
from around his neck, and slipped it into the lock.
Tom tried to turn the key, but it wouldn't budge.
As Tartok swam away from him, roaring with
anger, Tom gripped the key with all his strength.

He threw all his weight backward, bracing his
feet on the ice and snow. His shoulder burned with
pain as Tartok dragged him toward the edge of the
ice. Tom knew he was losing his grip. He needed
to act quickly, before he plunged into the freezing
water. He summoned all his strength, and twisted
the key one last time.

The lock unclasped and the collar broke apart in
a haze of golden light!

"Yes!" he shouted, tumbling backward. He placed the key back around his neck — and Tartok sank into the water without another sound.

Tom waited tensely for her to resurface, but the water that had swallowed her remained still. The warm sun disappeared behind gray clouds, and the temperature started to plummet once again.

Then Storm reared up in fright as the ice was smashed open beneath Elenna's feet — and as Tartok pulled herself out, Elenna fell into the shimmering deep.

"No!" cried Tom in horror.

But Tartok dove straight back into the water, and a few moments later she returned — holding a spluttering and shivering Elenna in her arms.

"Put her down!" Tom shouted.

Tartok placed Elenna gently on the ice at Storm's hooves. Then she swung around to face Tom. Her eyes were no longer red, but a glittering, icy blue.

For a long moment, Tom and the Beast looked at each other. Tom drew in his breath. Even though he knew she was free of Malvel's spell, her sheer size and power terrified him.

Tartok stared at the boy who had freed her, and then abruptly turned on her heel. With a powerful and yet graceful stride, she disappeared into the distance.

Tom gazed after Tartok and felt flush with pride. Another Beast had been freed from Malvel's evil spell. Tom knew how lucky he was to survive this Quest. He'd come face-to-face with the kingdom's most powerful creatures and lived to tell about it — so far, at least.

Tom shook himself free of his thoughts. Elenna was shivering violently on the bank, teeth chattering so hard she couldn't speak, her skin blue with cold. The cut on her forehead looked black, surrounded by a purple bruise. Tom pulled off his coat of furs and wrapped it around her.

"C-c-cold," she said faintly.

"I know," he said. "We need to get you warmed up."

Elenna clutched his arm. "You set Tartok free?"

"Yes. Now try to rest."

"I hope Shah finds her way back home," Elenna whispered. "I — I promised I'd take her back."

"You will," he said. "We'll find her and everything will be all right, you'll see."

Tom tried to smile, but inside he was starting to panic. He had given the blankets on his sleigh to Albin, and there was nothing else there of use. Soon night would fall — and without shelter or protection, soaked wet like this in the deathly cold — could Elenna survive the night?

CHAPTER TEN

THE HEALING

A LOUD WHINNY MADE TOM LOOK UP. STORM was standing at the top of the snowy rise, staring out toward the east.

"Storm!" Tom exclaimed.

Storm whinnied again, tossed his mane, and stamped one of his front hooves on the ground. Tom had a feeling that the stallion was trying to draw his attention to something.

"I'll be back in a moment," Tom told the shivering Elenna, and quickly climbed up the dune.

From there, Tom could see down onto an ice field. There were figures on horseback towing sleighs, moving over the plains. They must have blankets and shelter. "Well done, Storm," Tom said. These people were his only hope of saving Elenna.

"Hey!" he yelled. "We need help! Please, can you help us?" But even as he shouted, he knew that he was too far away. The people would never hear him. Tom looked down the slope and knew it was too steep for Storm. "Stay with Elenna, boy. I'm going to get help!"

When he'd set Tagus the Night Horse free, Tom had placed a sliver of the Beast's horseshoe in his shield. That had given him the power of speed and swiftness — and he needed it now.

Tom jumped onto the shield and rode it down the steep side of the snow dune. But once he'd reached the bottom, he found he wasn't slowing down. In fact, he was picking up speed! The shield's powers were working! Soon he was

racing across the frozen ground on his shield toward the people crossing the ice. The wind was bitingly cold, especially in just his woolen tunic, but he was too intent on reaching the strangers to really notice.

"Please, somebody help!" he yelled when he was finally close enough for them to hear.

The people stopped. They looked at Tom in surprise as the shield slowed down and he jumped off it.

"My friend fell into a split in the ice over in the dunes. She will die of exposure unless I can . . ." Then he gasped in surprise — one of their horses looked very familiar. "Hey, that's Shah. You found Shah, he belongs to Brendan's wife!"

"He was running wild," a man explained. "We thought he must have escaped from Brendan's camp. We are on our way there now."

"But, first, a small detour." A woman with a weathered face and long black hair gestured for

Tom to sit beside her on her sleigh. "It sounds like your friend needs help quickly."

Tom jumped aboard. "Are you from the clan camping in the east, in Rolaz?"

The woman barked a command at her horse and they sped off. "We were. But the land is not safe anymore. My name is Jennal, clan chief. I wish to ask Brendan's clan if we may join with them in Avantia."

Tom would have laughed at his good luck if he weren't so worried about Elenna.

They soon reached the valley where Elenna lay trembling. Jennal made her warm and comfortable with dry clothes and thick, woolen blankets, and her herbal treatments brought a healthy color back to Elenna's cheeks in minutes.

"I told you it would be all right," said Tom, squeezing his friend's cold hand.

She squeezed his fingers back and smiled.

*   *   *

Elenna was soon warm and comfortable on a sleigh, and Tom was riding Storm alongside Jennal.

The ice fields were cracked all over from the damage Tartok had done while under Malvel's evil spell.

"It's nothing to worry about," Jennal said, noticing Tom's concern. "In time, the ice will mend itself and all will be right in the northern plains. Until then, we can take an older route that is still passable."

It was true. The split that had cut them off from Brendan and the others would soon refreeze. With Tartok no longer breaking up the ice, the channel from Avantia to Rolaz could be traveled once again.

Night gathered over the desolate plains as the clan sped onward. Then, at last, they approached the wooden fence that marked the edge of Brendan's camp. Silver came racing out, yapping and barking with delight. Jennal's people looked alarmed for a moment.

Tom quickly explained: "It's only Silver, Elenna's pet."

Silver ran straight up to where Elenna lay on the sleigh and started licking her face and nuzzling her ear, his plumy tail wagging hard enough to fall off. Elenna laughed weakly. "It's all right, Silver, I'm feeling much better already."

"And so is everyone else, by the sound of it," said Tom. He could hear excited voices.

"Tom, Elenna!" cried Brendan, leaping the fence with a flaming torch in his hand. "I thought the split in the ice could not be passed!?"

Tom jumped down from Storm to greet him. "We took an older route."

"Is Albin feeling better?" Elenna asked.

"I'm fine!" called Albin, ducking under the fence. "I'm glad you're all right." He grinned at the sound of a familiar whinny. "And Shah's back safe, too!" Albin rushed to give the bay pony a hug.

"But who has brought you back to us safely?" Brendan peered into the gloom. "Is that Jennal?"

"Greetings, Brendan," said the clanswoman, crossing to meet him. "It seems times have been as hard for you as for us."

"I think perhaps our luck has turned," he said. Brendan smiled at Jennal. "Whatever wild animals roam these lands," he went on, "if you join us, together we will be strong enough to fend them off."

"Together we will prosper," Jennal agreed.

Brendan's eyes shone in the flickering light of the torch. "But first, you must be exhausted from your long journey. Let my people stable your horses and unload your things. Tonight we shall feast and celebrate the joining of our clans."

Everyone started to walk toward the camp, but Tom and Elenna lingered with Storm and Silver.

"A feast sounds wonderful," she said. "Can we stay?"

"I think we could both use a night's rest after today," Tom agreed.

Silver jumped up at Tom's legs, trying to get his attention. Turning, he saw a familiar misty glow that had appeared in midair. The glow slowly formed into the image of a white-haired man in a red cloak.

"Aduro!" Tom said. He knew the wizard was able to follow their progress from King Hugo's palace. "I wondered if you would come."

"You have acted bravely and fought well," the wizard told them. "Tartok is free to protect the northern people once again, and the kingdom's medical supplies will get through safely."

"I'm glad I could serve the kingdom," Tom said humbly. He wondered whether Tartok would provide another shield charm. Before Tom could ask, the wizard responded.

"And I believe Tartok left you something," Aduro told him, nodding in the direction of

Tom's shield. Tom flipped it over in his hands and sure enough, there it was — one of Tartok's claws. It must have come loose when she struck the shield.

"As the scale of the Dragon protects you from fire, so the claw will protect you from extreme cold." Aduro looked at them gravely. "But be warned. Magic alone is not strong enough to protect you from the fiercest Beast of all."

A shiver went through Tom. The Quest was not over.

Aduro nodded gravely. "You must journey to the Far East, where Epos the Winged Flame awaits you. This will be your greatest trial of all." Aduro glanced back at the camp. "But first, you must rest. Eat and drink to your fill. Build your strength for the long trek ahead — and for your battle with Epos." The wizard began to fade from sight. "Good luck . . ."

Then he was gone.

Storm whinnied quietly, and Silver looked up at his mistress.

"The fiercest Beast of all," Elenna echoed nervously.

"Let's not think about it tonight," said Tom. "Let's enjoy the feast and face the future tomorrow."

"Together," she smiled.

He nodded. "Always."

Happy sounds of talk and laughter, and the delicious smell of cooking were coming from the camp. Everyone was ready to celebrate.

Elenna went to join them. Tom started to follow, then paused and looked back over his shoulder at the kingdom of Avantia. New adventures waited for him out there. Was he strong enough to face them? Tom thought about his missing father — the father he wanted to be proud of him. "While there's blood in my veins," he swore to himself. Then he turned and walked into camp.

A Beast too big to defeat?

A phoenix of terrible power, Epos the Winged Flame, has been slowly awakening a long-dead volcano. If Tom and Elenna can't stop the Beast in time, it could mean a deadly eruption!

www.scholastic.com

BQ6